Beast Quest®

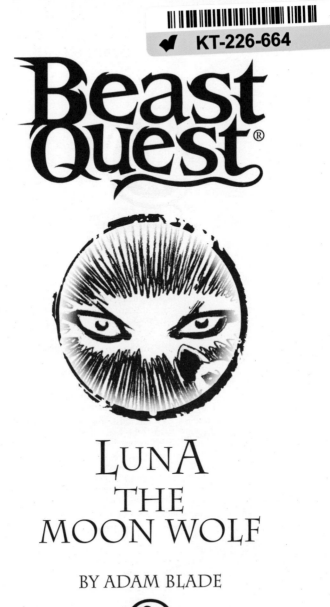

LunA
THE
MOON WOLF

BY ADAM BLADE

ORCHARD

WELCOME TO

Collect the special coins in this book. You will earn one gold coin for every chapter you read.

Once you have finished all the chapters, find out what to do with your gold coins at the back of the book.

With special thanks to Brandon Robshaw

For Elom Baka

www.beastquest.co.uk

ORCHARD BOOKS

First published in Great Britain in 2009 by The Watts Publishing Group
This edition published in 2015

5 7 9 10 8 6 4

Text © 2009 Beast Quest Limited.
Cover illustrations by Steve Sims
© Beast Quest Limited 2009
Inside illustrations by Brian@KJA-artists.com © Beast Quest Limited 2009

Beast Quest is a registered trademark of Beast Quest Limited
Series created by Beast Quest Limited, London

A CIP catalogue record for this book is available from the British Library.

ISBN 978 1 40834 820 8

Printed in Great Britain by Clays Ltd, Elcograf S.p.A.

MIX
Paper from
responsible sources
FSC® C104740

The paper and board used in this book are made from wood from responsible sources

Orchard Books
An imprint of Hachette Children's Group
Part of The Watts Publishing Group Limited
Carmelite House, 50 Victoria Embankment, London EC4Y 0DZ

An Hachette UK Company
www.hachette.co.uk
www.hachettechildrens.co.uk

CONTENTS

All hail, fellow followers of the Quest.

We have not met before, but like you, I have been watching Tom's adventures with a close eye. Do you know who I am? Have you heard of Taladon the Swift, Master of the Beasts? I have returned – just in time for my son, Tom, to save me from a fate worse than death. The Dark Wizard, Malvel, has stolen something precious from me, and until Tom is able to complete another Quest, I must wait between worlds, neither human nor ghost. I am half the man I once was and only Tom can return me to my former glory.

Will Tom have the strength of heart to help his father? This new Quest would test even the most determined hero. And there may be a heavy price for my son to pay if he defeats six more Beasts...

All I can do is hope – that Tom is successful and that I will one day be restored to full strength. Will you put your power behind Tom and wish him well? I know I can count on my son – can I count on you, too? Not a moment can be wasted. As this latest Quest unfolds, much rides upon it.

We must all be brave.

Taladon

PROLOGUE

Marina heard the cry of an owl.
Snowy!

She threw back the bedclothes and padded to the window. The sky was aflame with an orange sunset and she saw Snowy swooping over the fields, hunting for mice.

Marina never felt like sleeping on these long summer evenings.

I wish I was out there with Snowy,

she thought.

She crept to the top of the stairs. From behind the kitchen door, she heard the murmur of her parents chatting. She had a good hour before they would come upstairs. Long enough for a run in the fields with Snowy!

She tiptoed down the stairs and lifted the latch on the back door. The grass was damp beneath her bare feet and the evening breeze ruffled her hair. She ran over the fields towards her pet owl. Snowy saw her coming and swooped down, hooting a welcome.

"Hello, my friend!" Marina cried out. She held up her hand for him to perch on. But Snowy seemed to be in a playful mood. He soared away from her and flew across the field.

Marina laughed and ran after him. He was flying east, away from where the sun had already begun to dip below the horizon. The orange sky was darkening to a dusky pink.

"Snowy!" she called. "Snowy, come back!"

He was heading towards the ancient stone wall that marked the eastern edge of Avantia, where the Forbidden Land began. As she watched, he sailed over the wall. Then he disappeared.

Marina slowed down. What should she do? Her parents had always warned her that she must never enter the Forbidden Land. If she waited, perhaps Snowy would fly back.

Then she heard a squawk of distress. Snowy was in trouble!

Marina ran to the wall and began to climb. It was made of layers of dry stone with plenty of handholds.

She was a good climber, used to shimmying up the apple trees in her father's orchard.

She let herself down the other side of the wall and dropped lightly to the ground.

A huge forest stretched before her. In the rays of the dying sun the trees looked red, as if they were coated with blood. She touched the trunk of the nearest tree. It was wet and sticky – her hand came away covered in a thick red liquid.

She gave a scream of shock.

"Snowy!" she called out, her voice trembling. "Snowy, let's go!"

Then a high-pitched howl drifted

through the air and two burning red dots appeared between the trees.

A huge wolf with shaggy white fur emerged from the forest. Its eyes gleamed like burning coals; its lips peeled back to reveal curved yellow fangs, glistening with drool. As its glowing eyes fixed on Marina, the wolf reared back on its hind legs and howled again. Marina saw that the Beast's claws were black and fused together like knives.

The sun dropped below the horizon. The sky was a velvety dark blue, and a white full moon had risen above the forest.

Marina backed away, too scared to turn and run. Was the wolf about to pounce?

But as the moon continued to rise, the wolf grew pale. Now Marina could see the trees through its body. She realised her enemy was becoming transparent.

"Like a ghost," she whispered.

Then the wolf faded away completely. Nothing was left but the two burning red eyes, bobbing in the night air.

Marina felt an icy wind sweep towards her. Rustling noises came from the forest.

Snowy gave another squawk. Marina looked up to see him appear through the trees, flying high. He was alive! But as she watched, Snowy lost height. She could see his wings whip back against his body as

he dived through the air. He wasn't flying – he was falling!

He landed at Marina's feet. His feathers were torn and bloodied.

"Snowy!" she cried, falling to her knees beside her friend.

Gently, she cradled Snowy's broken body in her hands. As she climbed to her feet, a fox thrust its nose out of the trees. Then a badger. Another fox. A wild dog. Two hawks appeared in the sky, then a tawny owl, much larger than Snowy.

Animals were gathering at the edge of the wood. They were slowly advancing across the clearing.

"What do I do?" Marina whispered to herself. She heard the ghost-wolf howl for a third time. As one, the wild animals swarmed towards her.

Instinctively, she broke into a run. A wild dog tried to leap at her, but she scrambled up the wall at the edge of the Forbidden Land and dropped down into the damp grass on the other side. Cradling the dead owl's body in her arms, she ran back towards her home, while the screeching and hissing of furious animals filled the air behind her.

Before darting back into the house, she looked over her shoulder and saw the twin red eyes of the ghost-wolf, as it leapt into the air beyond the wall. She shuddered as she locked the wooden door and ran upstairs, back to her bed.

She should never have climbed the

wall into the Forbidden Land. Now her best friend was dead...

1

A LONG WAY DOWN

A cold wind moaned as Tom led the way down the steep, winding mountain path. Silver padded along at his heels, tongue lolling. Behind them, Elenna led Storm over the stony track, taking care to keep away from the edge.

On either side of the path a sheer cliff of rock fell away.

Tom glanced down.

"Be careful," he said. "Take it slowly."

Silver whined and licked Tom's hand.

"Don't worry!" said Elenna. "We don't want to break our necks, do we, Storm?" She patted the horse's side. "How will we recognise Luna? Your father didn't have time to tell us what sort of Beast she is."

Taladon had visited them after their victory over Rashouk the Cave Troll, to advise them about their next Quest. Tom was always filled with pride when he saw his father. There was just one problem – the Dark Wizard, Malvel, had used his evil magic to turn Taladon into a ghost.

If Tom and Elenna were successful in their Quest to recover the pieces of the Amulet of Avantia and break Malvel's evil spell, they would return Taladon to the land of the living.

And while there's blood in my veins, Tom thought to himself, *I won't give up. No matter how dangerous it gets.*

"He warned us we should try to meet Luna only in daylight, didn't he?" Tom said. "Maybe that's a clue."

They rounded a bend in the path and a view of the Forbidden Land opened before them. It was grey, bare and featureless. Tom shuddered. There was nothing but dusty rocks, dry fields and dead trees as far as he could see.

Silver whimpered.

"Nice, isn't it?" said Tom. "No wonder King Hugo forbids his subjects to come here!"

Elenna laughed. "He needn't bother! No one would come here unless they really had to."

"Let's stop a minute and see if we can get our bearings," said Tom. They had been walking all morning and needed to rest anyway. He took his flask from Storm's saddlebag and gave it to Elenna. She had a swig, then Tom took a long drink. He poured some of the water into a hollowed-out rock for Silver and Storm, who lapped it up gratefully.

Tom held out both his hands. "Map!" he called in a loud,

commanding voice.

A shimmering silver square appeared in the air in front of him. As he watched, lines began to form on its surface. Tom saw the Dead Peaks, the mountain path they were climbing down, and the great plain of the Forbidden Land beneath. At the foot of the plain was a dark forest named the Dark Wood.

And gleaming amid the Dark Wood was a tiny piece of silver amulet! Finding it would bring Tom one step closer to completing his Quest – and one step closer to restoring his father to full life and power. But he knew there would be a penalty. He would lose one of the magic powers given to him by the Golden Armour. *So be it,* thought Tom. *That's a price I'll gladly pay.*

"Look!" he said excitedly, pointing at the Dark Wood on the map. "There's the next piece of amulet!"

Elenna peered over his shoulder. Storm sensed the excitement and whinnied. Silver gave a short, sharp bark.

Tom gazed out over the landscape, shading his eyes with his hand.

In the distance he could just make out a dark mass of trees. He pointed to it.

"That looks like the Dark Wood!" he said. "Let's check."

From his pocket he pulled out the magic compass his uncle had given him. It showed two possible directions – *Destiny* or *Danger*. He held the compass in front of them. At once the needle swung round and pointed.

Destiny.

"No doubt about it," said Tom. "That's where we must go."

"It's a long way," said Elenna. "We won't get there before tomorrow. It'll take us the rest of the day to get down this mountain."

Tom put the compass back in his pocket.

"We don't have that long," he said. "My father's life depends on us. We've got to find a faster way to get down the mountain!"

"And break our necks?" Elenna asked. She was right. Tom would

be protected if he fell by the feather
given to him by Arcta the Mountain
Giant, many Quests ago. But the
others would be in grave danger.

Tom gazed down the sheer slope
of the mountain, thinking hard.
Suddenly, he snapped his fingers as
an idea flashed into his mind.

"I know just what we need to do,"
he said, turning to his friend.

A DANGEROUS CLIMB

"What's the shortest distance between two points?" asked Tom.

"A straight line," said Elenna.

"Right," said Tom. "So the quickest way off this mountain is...?"

"Straight down!" said Elenna, a smile brightening her face. "But how?"

"You've got a rope, haven't you?"

33

Tom asked.

Elenna delved into her quiver and brought out a coil of rope, thin but strong. Tom glanced at a boulder lying on the path. "Perfect! We can tie one end of the rope around that rock."

Elenna passed the rope around the boulder and double-knotted it. She tugged to make sure the rope held firm, then nodded at Tom. He went to the edge of the path and looked down. The cliff face was a sheer drop. Far below, he could see where the path, a tiny wiggly line, emerged onto the lower slopes.

"What about the animals?" said Elenna, glancing over at Storm and Silver, who were waiting patiently.

"Without us they can go much faster," said Tom. "They can follow the path and meet us at the bottom."

"Are you sure the rope's long enough?" asked Elenna.

"There's only one way to find out," Tom told her. He flung the rope over the edge of the cliff. They heard the *whoosh* of it snaking through the air. Tom and Elenna peered down and saw the end swinging far below.

"If we get to the end of the rope and it's too far to jump down to the ground," said Elenna, "we'll be stuck. We won't have the strength to climb all the way back up again."

Tom knew Elenna was right, but he wasn't about to give up now. "I'll go first," he told his friend.

He grasped the rope, turned round and lowered himself over the side. Silver peered down at him inquisitively, as if he were trying to figure out what Tom was doing.

"The moment of truth," said Tom, grinning up at Elenna. He hoped he looked braver than he felt.

He swung out from the cliff face,
dangling in empty air. The effort
of clinging to the rope turned his
hands white, but he managed to get
it gripped between his knees. That
felt more secure! Slowly, he made his
way down, hand over hand.

Tom looked up and saw Elenna,
Storm and Silver all peering over the
top of the cliff, watching him.

"Don't get too close to the edge!"
he called. Then he stared straight
ahead at the cliff face.

His arms ached and his muscles
trembled. *Come on, you can do this,*
he told himself. An icy wind blew
and the rope swayed dangerously.
Tom felt himself being blown into

the rock face. *No!* He couldn't put out his hands to protect himself and he smashed his head into a jutting piece of rock. A warm trickle of blood ran down his cheek. He breathed slowly, allowing the strength of heart given to him by the golden chainmail to return.

After a few breaths, Tom felt ready to carry on. He found a rhythm: grip with the right hand, slide the left hand down; grip with the left hand, slide the right hand down; grip with both hands, slide the knees down; grip with the right hand...

His hands were numb.

"It's not far now, Tom!" Elenna called. "You can do it!"

He risked a glance down. The slope

wasn't too far below – the drop was about the length of a medium-sized tree. But the rope didn't reach. Not even nearly.

What could he do?

Jump?

Then Tom noticed an outcrop of rock just below him. If he could land on it, he would be able to scramble down the rest of the way.

There was nothing else for it.

Tom took a deep breath and let go of the rope. He felt himself falling through the air, weightless. Then his feet hit the rock, jarring his ankles. He staggered – and just managed to right himself in time. He pressed his back against the cliff.

That was close! he thought. He dropped to his hands and knees and scrambled over the side of the rock, feet first. Then he took a deep breath and launched himself into the air, hitting the packed earth hard. His knees buckled, sending him rolling through the dirt.

Made it! he thought jubilantly.

"Tom! Are you all right?" called
Elenna. Her face was a tiny white
oval from this distance.

Tom climbed stiffly to his feet.

"I'm fine!" he shouted back.

"Your turn!"

Elenna began to climb down.
Tom watched with his heart in his
mouth. When she got to the end of
the swaying rope, he called out

to her. "Just underneath there's a bit of rock that sticks out. It's big enough to stand on. Can you see it?"

"Yes," said Elenna.

She hit the rock and reeled. Tom gasped as he saw her stagger, off-balance, right over the edge of the rock. He threw himself forwards and caught her in both arms. Elenna's weight knocked him to the ground. They both rolled over then sat up, covered in dust but smiling.

"Thanks!" said Elenna, straightening her quiver.

"No problem," said Tom.

Elenna whistled up to Silver. The sound carried clearly in the thin air. Alert as always, Silver understood what to do. Tom saw him pad to where the rope was tied. A few moments later it came snaking down to Tom and Elenna.

"I trained him to gnaw through knots one time," Elenna explained.

"I never thought I'd need to use that trick again." She re-coiled the rope and placed it in the bottom of her quiver.

High above, Storm and Silver set off down the twisting path at full speed. Soon Tom and Elenna saw the two animals appear round the corner, running quickly.

"Well done!" said Tom, patting Storm's neck. Elenna ruffled the fur on Silver's head.

"We don't have time to rest," she said. "We must keep moving."

They were on the edge of the plain now. The Dark Wood could clearly be seen, no more than half a day's walk away. As Tom gazed at the distant treetops, a shiver passed over him.

"We're getting close, Elenna," he said. "And Luna is waiting for us."

CROSSING THE FORBIDDEN LAND

They made their way over the dry and dusty plain. For a long time, the Dark Wood appeared to get no closer. Tom felt stupid with tiredness. His legs ached. He glanced at Elenna, she looked every bit as tired as he felt.

Her skin was covered with a fine film of dust and her face appeared pinched and sharp. Storm and Silver trotted on gamely, but even they were panting hard. Daylight was fast fading.

"We have no choice. We need to stop and rest," said Tom. "And we need to drink something."

Elenna took out her flask and shook it. The faint sloshing noise showed how little was left. Tom knew his own flask didn't hold much more.

"We need to find water!" said Tom.

"Look!" said Elenna. "What's that?"

She was pointing to a clump of greenery a little way off. Tom saw a cluster of stunted bushes and grasses growing around a spring that bubbled up through the rocks.

It was the first sign of life they had come across in the Forbidden Land. They ran to the spring. The water was as clear as crystal, bubbling to the surface.

The animals gathered at the edge of the water. Tom knelt down by the pool and scooped the cool liquid into his hands. He brought it to his lips and took long, grateful gulps. The water was cold and fresh and sweet. Storm and Silver plunged in, throwing up a spray of crystal droplets, and lapped until their thirst was quenched. Elenna waded in and splashed water over the rest of them.

"It's so cold!" she cried.

"Just what we need!" said Tom.

He washed off the remnants of the mud and feathers they'd covered themselves with to disguise their scent when they battled Rashouk. It felt good to be clean again.

"I'm hungry," said Elenna, shaking the water out of her hair.

Tom nodded. "We should eat, then rest. But there's not much – just a few biscuits—"

"Leave it to me!" said Elenna. She climbed out of the spring and took the bow from her quiver. Then she fitted an arrow to it. "You get a fire going, and I'll find something to cook on it."

She strode off over the plain with Silver at her heels. Tom went to collect some dried grass, twigs and larger sticks. He laid the grass and twigs on a flat rock. Then he rubbed two of the dry sticks together. He rubbed until his hands ached – but at last his efforts were rewarded. A thin spiral of smoke rose up from the sticks. A spark jumped and the dry grass caught at once.

Tom carefully fed the flames with the smaller sticks, then the larger ones. The blue-grey smoke rose into the sky. The fire was crackling nicely by the time Elenna returned carrying two large birds. Tom and Elenna cooked the birds over the flames, turning them on long sticks. The aroma of roasting meat made Tom's mouth water. He'd never smelt anything so good!

The birds tasted as delicious as they smelt. Elenna threw chunks of meat to Silver, who snapped them up greedily. Storm cropped the grass that grew around the spring.

"That feels better," said Tom. It was beginning to get dark now, and their fire glowed more brightly. He yawned. "Let's get some rest. We'll need all our strength tomorrow to face Luna."

"You're right," said Elenna, stretching her arms above her head. "Good night!" She drew her cloak around herself and lay down on the ground. Silver settled beside her, curling his body close to hers. Storm stood a little distance away, his head bowed.

Tom lay down and closed his
eyes. But sleep wouldn't come. He
couldn't help thinking about the
powers that had deserted him over
the past three Quests. He had lost
his ability to leap great heights, his
magic sword skills and the power
to run extra fast. Piece by piece, his

skills were deserting him as Taladon was returned to his true self. Tom knew that next he would lose the magic given to him by the golden breastplate – the power to lift huge weights.

I'm being stripped of my special skills, he thought, *turning over on the hard ground. Will I be able to carry on defeating these Beasts?*

He sat up, watching the flickering flames of the fire. He heard the breeze whispering through the grasses, then other noises – rustling, as though small animals were scurrying about nearby. Snuffling. The tread of paws.

He peered into the darkness, but could see nothing beyond the circle

of light cast by the fire. Then a
sudden sound pierced through him
like a knife.

The high, drawn-out howl of
a wolf.

It was nearby. Tom smelt a musky,

hairy animal smell, like Silver's
scent but far stronger. He stood up,
his hand on the hilt of his sword.
His heart was thudding in his
chest. Then he saw, glowing in the
darkness, two fiery red dots.
Close together, like eyes. They were
coming nearer.

Something was out there – and it
was heading straight for Tom!

4

A DEADLY ATTACK

Moving quickly, aware of the
glowing red eyes watching him,
Tom ran over to where Elenna lay
sleeping. As he did so, he caught
a glimpse of what lay just beyond
the firelight. There, in the semi-
darkness, a host of wild animals
lurked. There were foxes, badgers,
rats and wild dogs. Tom saw their
bared teeth glimmer in the darkness.

And behind them, those two red eyes, like burning embers. They were getting closer.

"Elenna!" Tom hissed. Silver sprang to his feet. His legs were straight and stiff, his fur bristling on end. He planted himself in front of Tom. His black lips were wrinkled in a snarl, his long fangs exposed. A deadly glint of threat lurked in his eyes. Tom had never seen Silver like this.

The growl in the wolf's throat deepened, becoming even more threatening.

"Hey, Silver, it's me," said Tom. "What's the matter?"

"What is it?" said Elenna, awaking with a start. Silver flattened his belly to the ground.

He's going to spring! thought Tom.
Then Silver flew through the air
towards him.

Tom tried to leap to the side. Too
late, he remembered that he no
longer had the power of the golden
boots, which had allowed him to

jump enormous distances. Silver smashed into Tom's chest and the weight of the wolf knocked him to the ground. They rolled over and over together in the dust. The animal scent of Silver's fur filled Tom's nostrils.

"Silver!" Tom heard Elenna cry. "Stop!"

Tom found himself lying on his back. He could feel the powerful muscles rippling beneath Silver's coat. The wolf's slavering jaws were a hand's breadth from his face. Desperately, he managed to get his arms up to ward the wolf off. Silver's teeth sank into the soft leather of his jerkin.

Storm neighed in alarm.

"Silver! No!" shouted Elenna. She grabbed Silver by the scruff of the neck and tried to drag him away. Silver snarled and turned to snap at her. His fangs only just missed her hand.

"Stay back!" panted Tom. "He's gone wild!" Beyond Elenna, he could see the eyes of the forest animals, glittering in the light from the campfire as they watched and waited. How long did Tom have before they attacked, too?

Thinking fast, Tom unbuckled his sheathed sword and pushed it in to Silver's face, holding him at bay. The wolf snarled furiously. Tom looked into his eyes, and saw nothing but rage. What had happened to their friend? He gripped the sword more tightly, forcing Silver's muzzle away from him.

"Silver!" shouted Elenna. She grabbed him by the fur on his back and tried again to drag him away. The enraged animal shook her off.

Tom saw that the creatures

encircling them were growing bolder. Rats, foxes, badgers and wild dogs advanced, snorting and growling.

"Elenna – keep those animals away!" gasped Tom.

His friend snatched up a flaming branch from the fire and thrust it at the creatures. They backed away, snarling.

The strange red eyes were moving in the dark, circling the campfire. As they came closer, Tom realised that the eyes were the only part of this animal that was visible. The campfire didn't light up any fur or muscles, and Tom couldn't see claws or teeth. *It must be the Beast!* Tom knew from Aduro and Taladon that all the Beasts on this Quest had the ability to change into ghostly form.

Luna gave another wolfish howl. From the other side of the fire, more dogs and foxes came forwards, snarling. Silver launched himself at Tom again, even more ferociously.

The Beast is controlling the animals, Tom realised. *They're doing her bidding, she's making them attack. Silver too.*

Storm ran at the wild animals, stamping his hooves. They shrank back, then regrouped. Luna howled again. More wild animals darted forwards. They were coming from all sides now, and the flaming branch was knocked from Elenna's hands as she tried to fight back a large dog.

She cried out as she was thrown to
the ground.

She twisted round to look at Tom
and he could see the fear in her eyes.

He reached out his free hand
towards her, but Silver launched a

new, frenzied attack. He ripped the sword from Tom's hands with his teeth and threw it to one side.

Tom heard it clatter to the ground beyond the light of the fire. Then Silver threw his full weight onto Tom, covering him with his body and smothering his face with his thick fur. Tom struggled beneath the wolf, but felt the fight draining out of him.

Silver's teeth flashed in the moonlight as he lunged closer. Tom turned his head away and felt the wolf's hot breath as the animal writhed on top of him, his claws tearing into Tom's flesh.

"No, Silver!" he cried. But when he turned his head back round, he saw a light in Silver's eyes that didn't belong there. It was the glow of evil.

There was nothing he could do now. If Silver wanted him dead, Tom didn't stand a chance.

SILVER IS SNARED

"Hold on!" cried Elenna, scrambling to her feet.

A rat threw itself at Tom's legs and he was just able to kick it away before its teeth sank into his thigh.

He was still pinned to the ground by Silver. He glanced over to see his friend dragging the rope from her quiver. Her hands moved rapidly, creating loops and knots.

"Hurry!" gasped Tom. Storm had cantered over and reared up on his back legs to keep the rest of the wild dogs, foxes and other vicious creatures at bay.

"There!" said Elenna. In one quick movement, she threw something over Silver's back. She'd knotted the rope into a loose net! Silver snarled and bucked, trying to shake the net off. But the more he struggled, the more entangled his paws became.

Now that Silver was distracted, Tom had the chance he needed.

With a mighty effort, he rolled out from under the wolf. His knee struck something.

It was his sword! Tom snatched it up, unsheathed it, and with all his force thrust the blade through one of the loops of the net, deep into the ground. Now the net was pegged down, but only in one corner. Silver was still struggling and might free himself at any moment.

Elenna fitted an arrow to her bow and aimed it at the opposite side of the net.

Thunk!

Silver howled in anger.

Thunk!

Thunk!

In rapid succession, Elenna sent two more arrows into the earth, pegging the net down securely. Silver was trapped. He jerked and kicked, trying to thrust his muzzle through the loops. But there was no way out.

His struggles gradually subsided and he lay still, panting. He was defeated.

Storm whinnied. Tom turned to look at the wild animals that surrounded them. With the defeat of Silver, their excitement had died down. They retreated a little, back into the darkness. Luna's burning red eyes still shone as the Beast slowly encirlced the camp.

Tom let out a shaky breath as he refastened his sword belt. "That was…close!"

Elenna stared at Tom in bewilderment. "I don't understand," she said. "I've never seen Silver behave like this!"

"It's not his fault," Tom reassured her. "It's the Beast's magic – she sent Silver mad."

"The Beast?" Elenna asked with a start, looking around.

"Can't you see the eyes?" Tom said, pointing. The twin red coals still burned in the darkness. But as Tom and Elenna watched, the eyes receded. Then they vanished.

"Should we chase after Luna?" said Elenna.

Tom looked at Silver. He shook his head. "We have more important things to deal with."

They sat down next to the wolf. Elenna put her hand on his back, stroking his fur through the net. He twitched and growled.

"Do you think he'll be all right again?" she asked anxiously.

"I hope so," Tom said. "All we can do is wait."

Above their heads, a white moon sailed through tatters of cloud. Storm snorted and stamped. The wild animals surrounding them finally melted away into the darkness.

Tom and Elenna watched the fire die down.

"I wonder," said Elenna after a while, "why Luna only sent Silver mad. Why not Storm as well?"

Tom scratched his head. "Silver – and those animals that came out of the forest – they're all wild predators. Storm is a bred and trained animal. And…well, Silver's a wolf." Tom remembered the eerie wolf howls that had rung out from the invisible Beast.

"So is Luna!" said Elenna. "That would explain why Luna had the power to control him!"

"That's what we're up against," said Tom sombrely. "A wolf like no other. Capable of turning wild animals even wilder."

"Why didn't she attack us herself?" Elenna wondered.

"I'm not sure. Maybe this was just a warning. To scare us off."

"But we won't be scared off!" Elenna said, driving a fist into her open palm.

"No," said Tom quietly.

Worn out by the fight, they both dropped off to sleep.

Tom woke early. The sky was lightening in the east. The sun showed over the horizon.

Silver whimpered. Elenna reached out to stroke him through the net.

This time Silver didn't growl, but whined softly.

Elenna turned to Tom. "What do you think? Is it safe to let him free?"

"Let's try it," said Tom. Together, they pulled the arrows from the ground. Tom uprooted his sword and sheathed it at his belt.

He and Elenna looked at each other. Then they each grabbed a corner of the net and eased it away.

Silver didn't move at first. He seemed utterly exhausted – as weak as a newborn puppy. But after a moment he turned his head and looked at Tom. All the fury had gone out of his eyes. He appeared subdued and even slightly ashamed. He inched forwards and put his head in

Elenna's lap. Elenna stroked him.

"There, there," she whispered comfortingly. Silver licked her gently on the arm.

Tom climbed to his feet and looked out to where the Dark Wood lay, still shrouded in shadow. That was where he was destined to encounter Luna again – it was where she was headed, Tom was sure. He and Elenna would go after her. And next time, he knew, the encounter would be more testing still.

"You won't beat me," he said into the dawn air. Luna would not get the better of him a second time.

THE DARK WOOD

They breakfasted on apples and water from the spring. Silver didn't eat anything, not even the biscuit Elenna tried to tempt him with. He lapped a little water, then lay with his head on his front paws.

"He's still not himself," said Elenna.

The fight had taken the energy out of Tom, too. He felt shaky.

"Well, we need to get moving anyway," he said. "Luna arrived last night when the moon was high in the sky. We have to face her before the moon comes up again, Elenna. It's the only chance we have of defeating her."

Storm neighed, as if in agreement.

There was no time to waste. Tom and his friends headed towards the Dark Wood. Elenna rode in Storm's saddle and Tom and Silver walked alongside them. Soon, the huge wood reared up, dark and ominous. The trees seemed to have a reddish tinge.

It was still light when they reached the edge of the Dark Wood, but only just. The sun was getting low in the sky. When Tom glanced back to see

the distance they had travelled, he
noticed their shadows streaming out
behind them. Ahead, the sun's rays
made the trees look even redder – a
bright, glistening crimson.

"Ugh!" said Elenna, dismounting.
"It looks like blood!"

"It's just an illusion," said Tom. "A
trick of the light. Come on, let's go.
Luna's in there – and we must find
her before it gets dark!"

Tom shifted his shield on his back

and gripped the hilt of his sword. Then they stepped into the wood.

Twigs and dry leaves crackled underfoot. The trees grew close together, and as Elenna passed between two of them, she put out a hand to steady herself. She cried out in disgust.

"What? What is it?" said Tom, pushing through the undergrowth.

"My hand! Look!" Elenna gasped.

Tom stared. Her hand was covered in sticky, glistening red blood! And all the other trees were coated in the same liquid.

They had stepped into a forest of gore.

Tom shuddered. Storm was whinnying uneasily, and Silver

whimpered.

"We need a plan," Tom said, looking around him. "You can feel the evil magic in this place. And we've got to face a giant ghost wolf with supernatural powers in here! We need something to fall back on. A place to run to, a way out, something to protect ourselves with—"

"Or a weapon," interrupted Elenna.

"Yes!" said Tom. She was right. He had his sword and Elenna had her bow, but he knew that would not be enough. Against such a formidable enemy they would need something extra. Something unexpected.

He stepped back out from the wood and scanned the arid plain of the

Forbidden Land. Was there anything there they could use?

But there was nothing. Just dusty earth, a few rocks and dry grass that was barely alive.

Twilight was descending. Time was running out.

From among the bloodstained trees of the Dark Wood, Tom thought he could hear noises. Faint, intermittent sounds, but gradually growing stronger. Scuffling, snuffling, rustling. And there! His heart thumping, Tom was sure he had heard the lonely howl of a wolf in the distance, echoing through the trees.

The sun was setting, and the Dark Wood was coming alive.

7

A NEST OF WOLVES

Tom listened to the rustling noises coming from the Dark Wood, and a memory surfaced. Back in his home village of Errinel, there was sometimes trouble from wild animals – foxes and the occasional wolf. In winter, when food was scarce, they would creep into the village by night and take hens, lambs and goats. The village elders' solution was to dig a deep, wide trench around the village and fill it with brambles. Tom recalled helping out the digging parties.

"How about if we dug a pit?" he said. "If we could lure Luna towards it..."

"...we might trap her!" finished Elenna. "Yes, it could work. But what can we dig with?"

"How about this?" said Tom. He dug the pointed end of his shield into the ground and shovelled up a chunk of earth. The ground was dry and hard, but once the surface was broken, the earth beneath was easy to dig.

With the strength given to him by the golden breastplate, Tom quickly shifted the earth. He had soon hollowed out a fair-sized crater.

"Let's see if I can find something to help with!" said Elenna. She went to the outskirts of the Dark Wood and fetched a broken branch, stout and strong, with a scooped end.

They fell into a rhythm, alternating their digging. Every now and then Elenna stopped to take a breather. Thanks to his magic strength, Tom dug tirelessly, without a pause. The hole widened and deepened. Soon they were both standing in a pit, throwing the earth over their shoulders.

Storm and Silver came to the edge, peering down at them curiously.

"That'll have to do!" said Tom.

"It's almost dark." He interlaced his fingers so that Elenna could use his hands as a foothold and scramble out. Then she let down the rope so he was able to climb free.

Working fast, they placed slender branches across the top of the pit and covered them with reddish leaves. No Beast would ever know a trap was waiting.

"This might be just the advantage we need," Tom said, gazing down at their work. The moon was out now. It was full, but not at its brightest, and not yet high in the sky. Twilight lingered above the trees.

Tom flashed a glance at Silver, who sat patiently beside Elenna.

"I know what you're thinking," said Elenna, as she took Silver by the scruff of the neck and pulled out the rope once more. She knelt in the grass and looked into her pet's eyes.

"I have to do this," she told Silver, as she tied the wolf to a tree trunk. With a sigh, she climbed to her feet and Tom put a hand on her shoulder.

"Thank you," he said. "I know how difficult that must have been for you. But we can't risk what might happen if Silver comes under Luna's spell a second time."

Elenna nodded sadly. Tom released a long, drawn-out breath. "Let's go and defeat this Beast," he said. "It's time."

Warily, they stepped into the Dark Wood. Tom and Elenna led, Storm following close behind. They took care to avoid touching the bloodied trunks of the trees. Tom could feel menace pressing upon him. The wood was quiet now. The only sounds were their own footsteps and the occasional snort from Storm. It was as if the whole wood was listening to them.

There was no sign of Luna. Yet Tom felt sure that she must know they were coming. *Perhaps she's waiting for the moon to rise to its full height?* he thought. *Then he heard a noise.*

He touched Elenna's arm and she stopped. Storm drew to a halt behind them.

"What is it?" mouthed Elenna silently.

Tom lifted his finger to his lips. They stood still, waiting.

The noise came again. A high-pitched yelp. And another. And another.

Elenna nudged Tom and pointed.

There, half-hidden beneath the gnarled roots of a tree, was a bundle of fur. Tom saw damp snouts poking out, pointed ears, and several tiny pairs of gleaming red eyes.

It was a nest of wolf cubs. Their scent was carried to him on the evening breeze, the same strong, musky animal scent he had smelt the previous night.

Tom and Elenna drew closer. They had seen a nest of wolf cubs before, when they went to do battle with Arcta. Those cubs had been cute, with blunt round faces and big paws. But these cubs looked ferocious. Their snouts were narrow, their eyes a fiery red, they glared at Tom and Elenna, snapping their jaws.

"They could be useful to us," breathed Tom. "They must be Luna's cubs – I'm sure of it! They have the same scent. The same red eyes. If we could get these cubs away from here, she'd follow, wouldn't she? Maybe we could lure her out of the wood. Then we could fight her in the open – where we might trap her in the pit!"

"If you try to pick those cubs up they'll take your hand off," warned Elenna.

But Tom wasn't going to be put off that easily. What would tempt such fierce creatures from their nest?

They clearly wanted to attack – he could use that to his advantage. "Watch," he said to Elenna.

Tom bent over the cubs. They growled and the largest cub leapt at him. Tom swiftly brought his shield up. The wolf cub's fangs crashed against its surface with such force he almost dropped the shield.

"Come on, then," he said, shifting the shield on his arm. "Come and get me!" The other cubs swarmed out of the nest. There were four of them in all. Yapping and snapping, they advanced on Tom.

And in the empty nest behind them, Tom saw something glinting in the moonlight. His heart jumped. He recognised the fragment of gold, with

the shard of blue enamel at
its heart.

"There, can you see it? It's a piece of
the amulet!" he called to Elenna.

"Can't we just grab it?" she cried.

Tom tried to circle round the cubs
so he could get to the nest, but they
rushed at him, their jaws snapping.
He was only just able to raise his
shield to protect himself.

"I can't get close to the nest!" he
shouted to Elenna. Desperation
coursed through him. The gold of the
amulet gleamed in the moonlight. If
Tom couldn't retrieve it, he would fail
in his Quest. And his father would
never be returned to life.

What was he going to do?

8

AN INVISIBLE ENEMY

"We have to get out of here," said Tom, "and fast. We'll come back for the amulet."

He began to back out of the forest. The cubs came after him in a pack, just as he'd planned. But it was a dangerous game that Tom had started. The cubs were fast, and they threw themselves at Tom from all sides. No sooner had he dodged one attack than he had to face another. Elenna tried to keep the cubs at a safe distance, using her bow to shoot arrows into the ground at their paws, but they looked determined to taste Tom's blood and nimbly leapt over the arrow shafts.

One of the cubs clamped its jaws on Tom's shield and hung there, growling. With difficulty he shook it off, and saw the deep marks its teeth had left in the wood. Immediately, he had to leap away from another cub trying to take a chunk out of his ankles.

"Nearly there!" Elenna encouraged him. She was by Tom's side, waiting for Luna to appear. She had a fresh arrow already fitted to her bow.

They passed the last of the bloodstained trees, with Storm following, and emerged out on the plain again.

It was completely dark now. High above, the full moon shone brightly.

Then Tom heard a sound that made the hairs at the back of his neck stand on end. The high, hungry howl of Luna.

At once the cubs froze. Tom saw his chance. He grabbed one of them by the scruff of its neck. It yowled in anger and the other three cubs relaunched their attack on Tom, scrabbling round his feet. But Silver leapt forwards, showing his fangs. The cubs backed off, growling defiantly.

The howl of the mother wolf rang out again – much closer this time. She was almost upon them. Tom stood with the cub in one hand and his shield in the other. Beside him, Elenna raised her bow. Storm paced the ground alongside them.

The Beast burst through the trees, looking round frantically for her young. Tom's plan had worked – he'd lured Luna out of the Dark Wood.

Elenna gasped. Tom instinctively took a step backwards.

He had never seen anything like this. More than three times the size of Silver, her fur was as white as the moon and her red eyes burned with fury. She spotted Tom and reared onto her hind legs. Her curved yellow fangs glistened with drool. Her claws were black, and fused together like knives.

Silver whimpered and slunk backwards. Storm stepped protectively in front of his friend.

Twang!

Elenna had loosed off an arrow.

It hit Luna's side and bounced away. Arrows were useless against her thick hide.

The three cubs on the ground bounded towards their mother. Tom let the cub he was holding drop, and it scampered back to Luna too. Tom drew his sword.

Luna dropped down onto all fours. A second later she was running over the plain towards Tom at blinding speed.

The Ghost Beast launched herself at Tom. He had a momentary glimpse of her narrow snout, burning red eyes and black claws sailing through the air towards him. He dived to one side.

The claws missed him by a hair's breadth.

Tom hit the ground, rolled and was up again. Already Luna had turned. She lunged at him, snapping. Tom just managed to get his shield up in time to protect himself, but the impact of Luna's weight nearly knocked it from his arm. He thrust his sword at the wolf, aiming for the centre of her chest. The blow was firm, but it didn't penetrate Luna's thick fur. The blade bounced off with a force that jarred Tom's whole arm.

Luna swiped at him with her curved black claws. The blow would have taken Tom's head off if he hadn't ducked in time.

He retreated, half-blinded by the sweat in his eyes, holding his shield before him. He saw Elenna loose off another arrow, this time aiming for the wolf's head. Again the arrow glanced off without doing any damage.

"I'm sorry, Tom," she called. "My arrows can't even scratch her!"

Luna leapt at Tom again. As he jumped aside, he slashed at her muzzle with his sword. He heard Luna howl in pain. He had managed

to hurt her – but not seriously.
He hadn't even drawn blood. All he'd
done was enrage her even more.

Her eyes glowed brighter still, and
she showed her teeth as she turned
and stalked towards Tom again.

Furiously, Luna opened her jaws
in a howl and arched her back as
she reared up on her hind legs. Tom
watched as she slowly became paler,
then transparent, as if she were
made of glass. Then she disappeared
completely. All Tom could see was
her two glowing red eyes. Now he
had to fight an invisible Beast! He
heard Elenna gasp as the eyes rushed
towards him.

Tom dived to one side. He felt the
snap of Luna's fangs just inches away

from his neck, her fur tickled his skin as she passed, even though he couldn't see her.

"I'll keep fighting you!" Tom yelled defiantly.

He got to his feet, holding out his shield and sword. He could see the red eyes bobbing in the air, but he had no idea from which direction Luna would attack. Behind him, he heard Storm pacing the ground.

Tom warily kept his sword up, making sure he was always facing the eyes as they hovered and circled him.

From the edge of the DarkWood, he heard the animal noises rising again – baying, snuffling, growling, howling.

"Tom!" shouted Elenna. "The wild animals are returning!"

Tom glanced over his shoulder and saw the black outlines of foxes, wolves and wild dogs at the edge of the forest. The moon had come out and now Luna was at her strongest. Time was running out for Tom.

He had to be brave and win this Quest – and he had to do it quickly.

THE FINAL FIGHT

"Elenna!" he called. "I'll deal with Luna. You and Storm try to keep the animals at bay!"

"We will!" she cried. She was already fitting another arrow to her bow. A flicker from Luna's burning red eyes warned Tom that the wolf was about to leap to the attack again.

Luna came back into full view. Tom saw her glittering white body and her black, knife-like claws hurtling through the air towards him.

He flung himself to the ground. Luna landed beyond him, snarling with anger. Tom was on his feet again in a flash.

He glanced up as the sky darkened even further, and saw that a huge, tattered cloud had passed over the moon. In the same moment, Elenna loosed an arrow, hitting one of the wild dogs in the side. It yelped and fled back into the wood. Storm advanced, driving the other animals back. *Luna's power over the animals fades when the moon's hidden!* Tom thought. *She has a weakness!*

Luna was stalking Tom, her red

eyes fixed upon him, her black lips curled back in a snarl. Her belly was close to the ground, she was clearly preparing to spring again.

Tom backed towards the secret pit he and Elenna had dug. He knew he couldn't keep dodging Luna's attacks for much longer. *Come on!* he thought. *Just a little further...*

Luna sprang. Tom saw the wolf's dripping fangs, her black, razor-sharp claws. He leapt towards the pit. Without the magic powers of the golden boots, which had helped him jump huge distances, he had to rely on his own ability to reach the other side of the hole.

Tom heard Luna howl triumphantly as she followed him.

He fell, rolled and turned...

Luna landed on the branches above the pit. They cracked beneath her weight. Her huge jaws opened in shock and rage. An anguished, furious howl burst forth as she crashed down, paws scrabbling helplessly, leaves and broken sticks flying up around her.

"Elenna!" shouted Tom. "Quick!"

Elenna was already running towards him.

"Help me cover her!" he said.

Tom was already furiously scooping earth down on the enraged Beast. Elenna joined in at once. The soil spattered on Luna's glittering white fur. With a defiant roar, the Beast half-raised herself from the

pit, struggling to escape. Tom would
never forget the sight: those red eyes
blazing up at him through the dirt.
Furiously, he and Elenna shovelled
more earth down on her.

But Luna seemed to find fresh

energy and heaved herself up, dirt pouring off her thick pelt. Her massive claws scrabbled at the side of the pit.

"Get out of the way!" Tom called to Elenna as they jumped to either side. Luna leapt into the air, her white fur glittering and her jaws snapping. But she fell onto the jagged end of a branch that had covered the pit. The point of the splintered wood pierced her chest and dark blood spurted across her fur. Luna let out a final defiant hiss and sank to the ground. Her eyes, which had glowed with evil, were closed. Tom and Elenna watched as the Beast's magic faded and she turned pale and transparent for the last time.

"We did it!" said Tom. They stood there, breathing hard, tired but triumphant. Storm came trotting over and Elenna ran to release Silver, who leapt around her as the two of them rejoined Tom and his stallion.

"I suppose she'll stay there forever now," said Tom. "The moonlight will never shine on her again." He heard a chorus of desolate howls. All the wild animals had fled back into the Dark Wood, except the four wolf cubs. They stood at the edge of the trees, howling at the moon. They had lost their evil mother. The sound sent shivers up Tom's spine.

THE NEXT QUEST

The cubs crept closer, sniffing the
air.

"What shall we do about them?"
asked Tom. He didn't like to see
Luna's young abandoned, even
though they had tried to attack him.
One of the cubs broke away from
the pack and came to sniff around
Elenna's feet, before looking up at
her with friendly eyes.

Elenna laughed and reached down to stroke the cub's head. He nipped playfully at her fingers, before darting back to join his siblings. They chased each other joyfully and ran back into the forest, barking encouragement to each other.

"They'll be all right," Elenna said. "Let them run wild. That's what they're born to do. They're old enough to fend for themselves."

"The amulet!" said Tom suddenly, as he realised the cubs' nest was now left unguarded. He set off at a run into the Dark Wood. Elenna, Storm and Silver followed.

Tom felt the change in the atmosphere as soon as he entered the forest.

"Look, Tom!" Elenna called. She put her hand to a tree trunk, but when she pulled it away it was no longer smeared in blood. There were just a few green streaks of moss across her palm. Tom smiled, and carried on striding through the undergrowth.

He could hear the noises of animals moving about, but there was nothing sinister or threatening about the sound now. The wood was wild, but, released from Luna's spell, it was no longer evil.

Tom found the nest again easily – a dark hollow beneath the roots of a gnarled tree, where the shard of gold amulet glinted in the moonlight. A sliver of blue winked at him from the fragment's edge. Carefully, he picked it up. It was heavy in his hand and his fingertips felt the inscription on the back of the precious metal.

The three other pieces of amulet Tom had gathered hung on a leather thong around his neck. He raised the fourth to join them. There was a gold catch that clicked into place with a satisfying sound. *Four pieces,* he thought. *Just two more to go.* With each new fragment, he was bringing his father closer to life.

"It's beautiful," said Elenna, as she caught up with him.

"Yes," said Tom softly.

Storm whinnied, as if in greeting. Tom looked up. His father, Taladon, was standing before them in a vision.

Taladon still looked ghostly. Tom could see the outlines of the trees through his body. But his strong, bearded face shone with pride as he looked at his son.

"Well done, Tom," he said in his deep voice. "I am proud to have a son who fights with such skill and courage."

Tom modestly lowered his gaze to the ground. "Well, I had a lot of help," he said.

"Yes." Tom looked back up to see Taladon's gaze pass to Elenna, and then to Storm and Silver. "My son is lucky to have such brave and loyal friends. Thanks to you all, I feel my powers returning."

As he said this, it seemed to Tom

that his father grew more solid than
before. The trees behind him became
less distinct. At the same time, he
felt a change in his own body – as
if energy was leaving him. By this
stage in the Quest, he understood
that another of the magical powers
he'd gained from the Golden Armour

had leaked away.

A fallen tree lay nearby in the forest. Tom went over to it. He bent down, placed both hands beneath it, and tried to lift.

Nothing happened.

He tried again, tugging with all his might. But the trunk was immovable. He straightened, breathing hard.

"I've lost my strength," he said. "The magic strength the golden breastplate gave me. It's gone!"

Taladon nodded gravely. "Every gain must bring some loss," he said. "And magical powers alone do not make a hero! It is the spirit that truly counts."

"Think of all the things you've done without magical powers," said

Elenna. "Like when you leapt over the pit so Luna would crash into it – that was a tremendous jump and you did it with no help. You're just as much of a hero without the Golden Armour – more so, because you're doing it all yourself!"

"Elenna is right," said Taladon. "You have shown true heroism on this Quest, Tom. And you will need to be even more of a hero on your next Quest."

Tom squared his shoulders. "I'll be ready for it," he said. "I'll do anything to bring you back to the land of the living."

"And you won't be alone!" said Elenna. "We'll be by your side!"

Silver gave a low howl of

agreement. Storm stamped and tossed his mane, eager to get going.

"Next you must face a very different Beast," said Taladon. "Blaze – a dark and deadly dragon!"

"A dragon?" Tom repeated. He remembered his first ever Quest, when he freed Ferno the Fire Dragon.

But his father was already growing indistinct. "I wish you well," Taladon said. For a moment, his outline hung in the air. Then he was gone.

"I won't be sorry to leave this place," Elenna said. She shuddered and turned to start walking out of the Dark Wood. As they emerged from the trees, they could see the

dry, dusty plain of the Forbidden
Land, with the mountains rearing up
in the distance.

Somewhere, far away, thought
Tom, *Blaze is waiting for us.*
Excitement coursed through him. He
was ready to face the next Beast.

"Let's go and find Storm and
Silver," he said, setting off down
the slope. There would be even

more difficult Quests to come, but whatever lay ahead of him, Tom knew he would do his best – for his friends and for Avantia.

CONGRATULATIONS, YOU HAVE COMPLETED THIS QUEST!

At the end of each chapter you were awarded a special gold coin.
The QUEST in this book was worth an amazing 11 coins.

Look at the Beast Quest totem picture inside the back cover of this book to see how far you've come in your journey to become

MASTER OF THE BEASTS.

The more books you read, the more coins you will collect!

Do you want your own
Beast Quest Totem?

1. Cut out and collect the coin below
2. Go to the Beast Quest website
3. Download and print out your totem
4. Add your coin to the totem
www.beastquest.co.uk/totem

Don't miss the next exciting Beast Quest book, BLAZE THE ICE DRAGON!

Read on for a sneak peek...

CHAPTER ONE

LEAVING THE FORBIDDEN LAND

The sun was just a finger's breadth over the horizon as Tom and Elenna left the Dark Wood. Tom was tired. The battle with Luna the Moon Wolf had tested him to the limit – and Elenna, too.

"Perhaps we should rest," she suggested.

Tom glanced at his friend. Her knees were scuffed from where she'd stumbled and fallen earlier. He then looked at their brave animal companions. Silver, Elenna's wolf, trotted on ahead with his head low, and Tom's horse, Storm, staunchly plodded forwards.

"I wish we could," Tom said regretfully. "But not yet."

He fingered the leather thong around his neck, from which hung the pieces of the Amulet of Avantia. So far he'd retrieved four amulet parts and defeated each of the Ghost

Beasts that had guarded them. But his Quest would not be complete until he had all six pieces, and the amulet was whole again. Only then would he be able to bring his father, Taladon, back for good.

His next Quest, so his father had told him, was to defeat a dragon called Blaze.

"Well, we need to stop and check the map," said Elenna. "We can drink some water at the same time."

Tom nodded and sat down on a boulder. Elenna took a flask from Storm's saddlebag and drank, while Tom stretched out his hand in front of him.

"Map!" he commanded.

The air rippled as the ghostly map

appeared. Without this gift from Aduro, they would never have been able to find their way through the Forbidden Land or locate the Beasts.

The map showed a glowing line, like a thread of gold, snaking from where they stood at the edge of the Dark Wood, across the eastern fields, past a small village called Rokwin, and towards the town of Stonewin. It ended on the slopes of the volcano.

"Stonewin is where Epos lives," said Elenna, handing Tom the flask.

"I hope she's not in danger from this dragon," said Tom, taking a swig of water. Epos the Flame Bird was their loyal friend; on another occasion they had saved her from Dark Wizard Malvel.

Tom placed a hand over his eyes and gazed in the direction of Stonewin. He called on the power to see across great distances given to him by the golden helmet, part of the suit of magical Golden Armour he had retrieved.

"There's the volcano at Stonewin,"

he said to Elenna. "But the crater isn't smoking. The volcano has smoked since the day I was born. Something's wrong."

"Then let's not waste any more time," Elenna insisted.

Now Tom had seen their Quest set out on the ghost map, strength returned to his heart, and they sped towards Avantian soil. As if sensing his urgency, Storm and Silver seemed to find new reserves of energy.

But even though his determination to complete the Quest was as strong as granite, worry tugged at Tom's mind. Each time he defeated one of Malvel's Ghost Beasts, one of his Golden Armour powers vanished.

Now he only had two left.

Tom shook his head. The people of Stonewin, and maybe even Epos herself, needed him. He would not let them down. He would not let Malvel win.

Tom and Elenna reached the high wall that separated the Forbidden Land from Avantia. They passed silently through the unmanned gate, back into familiarity.

"I'd forgotten that the sky could be so blue and the land so green," said Elenna. Storm whinnied and wheeled about, bolting off across the lush grass. Silver spun round in wild circles of joy.

"If we don't succeed in this Quest," said Tom, "Malvel's Beasts will take over Avantia, too – *everywhere* will be as dead looking as the Forbidden Land."

Read
BLAZE THE ICE DRAGON
to find out more!

FIGHT THE BEASTS,
FEAR THE MAGIC

Are you a BEAST QUEST mega fan?
Do you want to know about all the latest news,
competitions and books before anyone else?

Then join our Quest Club!

Visit the BEAST QUEST website
and sign up today!

www.beastquest.co.uk

Discover the new Beast Quest mobile game fro

Available free on iOS and Android

Guide Tom on his Quest to free the Good Beasts
of Avantia from Malvel's evil spells.

Battle the Beasts, defeat the minions,
unearth the secrets and collect
rewards as you journey through the
Kingdom of Avantia.

DOWNLOAD THE APP TO BEGIN
THE ADVENTURE NOW!